All Ladybird books are available at most bookshops,
supermarkets and newsagents, or can be ordered direct from:

Ladybird Postal Sales
PO Box 133 Paignton TQ3 2YP England
Telephone: (+44) 01803 554761
Fax: (+44) 01803 663394

A catalogue record for this book is available
from the British Library

Published by Ladybird Books Ltd
A subsidiary of the Penguin Group
A Pearson Company
© LADYBIRD BOOKS LTD MCMXCVIII

LADYBIRD and the device of a Ladybird are trademarks of
Ladybird Books Ltd Loughborough Leicestershire UK

Little
Red Hen

illustrated by Graham Percy

The wheat

The dog

The cat

The flour

Little Red Hen

The rat

The bread

"Will you help me plant the wheat?" asked Little Red Hen.

"No," said the rat, the cat and the dog.

"Then I will plant it all by myself," said Little Red Hen.

And she did.

"Will you help me
cut the wheat?"
asked Little Red Hen.

"No," said the rat,
the cat and the dog.

"Then I will cut it
all by myself," said
Little Red Hen.

And she did.

"Will you help me make the flour?" asked Little Red Hen.

"No," said the rat, the cat and the dog.

"Then I will make it all by myself," said Little Red Hen.

And she did.

17

"Will you help me make the bread?" asked Little Red Hen.

"No," said the rat, the cat and the dog.

"Then I will make it all by myself," said Little Red Hen.

And she did.

"Will you help me eat the bread?" asked Little Red Hen.

"Yes," said the rat,
the cat and the dog.

25

"No," said Little Red Hen. "I will eat it all by myself."

And she did!

Read It Yourself is a series of graded readers designed to give young children a confident and successful start to reading.

Level 1 is suitable for children who are making their first attempts at reading. The stories are told in a very simple way using a small number of frequently repeated words. The sentences on each page are closely supported by pictures to help with reading, and to offer lively details to talk about.

About this book

The pictures in this book are designed to encourage children to talk about the story and predict what might happen next.

The opening page shows a detailed scene which introduces the main characters and vocabulary appearing in the story.

After a discussion of the pictures, children can listen to an adult read the story or attempt to read it themselves. Unknown words can be worked out by looking at the beginning letter *(what sound does this letter make?)*, and deciding which word would make sense.

Beginner readers need plenty of encouragement.